The Amish Orphan's Christmas

Hannah Schrock

Born and Raised

Philadelphia, Pennsylvania, a few weeks before Christmas…

Holly Sanders turned her head as the voices of excited people came from the direction of the escalator. It was the week after Thanksgiving and the newspaper where she worked was decorated for the Christmas Season. Fake pine trees, decorated with every color and shape of ornament occupied spaces throughout the building, and Christmas music played across the speakers. The atmosphere amongst her fellow journalists was contagious, and even the dour-faced administrators seemed to be more relaxed and joyful today. She only wished she could find some joy for herself.

This would be the first Christmas she'd spend without being able to call and talk to her mother. They hadn't actually been all that close the last few years of her mother's life – a fact that hurt Holly immeasurably. It was all her fault and she'd lost track of the times she'd wished she could roll back time and do things differently.

At the age of twenty-two, she wasn't supposed to have so many regrets, and yet she did. Holly had left home three years earlier, not liking the fact that her mother refused to talk about her father, or tell her where to find him. She'd never met the man and the only information her mother had been willing to impart was his name. Brian Sanders. She'd also told her the last time she'd seen him they'd lived in Philadelphia.

Her mother, Sarah, had married Brian Sanders, but divorced him two months later. Brian had been extremely lazy, and an abusive man when he'd been drinking. Sarah had left him after finding out she was pregnant with Holly and never looked back. Holly could understand her mother not wanting to stay married to a man like that, but over the years, she'd become desperate to find the man who'd fathered her. To ask him if he'd changed and why he'd never tried to contact her.

Her mother had been adamant that Brian didn't deserve her attention, and shortly after turning nineteen, Holly and her mother had engaged in their final fight over the topic. Holly had packed up her belongings and headed to Philadelphia, in search of the father who'd been missing the last nineteen years of her life. Her mother had been hurt with what she saw as Holly's defection, but at the time, Holly had been singularly focused on finding her father. Her mother's hurt feelings weren't something she allowed herself to consider.

If she'd known how things would play out, she might have done things differently. She'd spent two months in Philadelphia looking for him, before she'd gone into the public library to do a name search. She'd been hoping to find some mention of Brian Sanders in the business pages of the newspaper, instead, she'd found his obituary. He'd died ten days before she'd arrived in Philadelphia of liver cancer, caused by his predilection to living an alcoholic lifestyle.

She'd been devastated, and had ended up discovering that her father was a frequent flyer at the local homeless shelter, his love for booze greater than his need to take care of himself most of the time. The woman at the shelter had suggested she try and mend fences with her mother and get on with her life. Advice Holly had only partially taken.

In her mind, she was sure she could have made a difference in her father's life, if only her mother had told her where to find him sooner. She'd thrown that accusation at her mother, who'd only remained silent and refused to discuss the subject. Their estrangement had continued and Holly had taken some night classes at the university and obtained a job as a low-level journalist with a local newspaper.

She'd placed the perfunctory phone calls to her mother on Christmas, Mother's Day, and her mom's birthday, but a wall had been erected between them and they were neither one willing to swallow their pride. Holly still blamed her mother for keeping her away from her father, a man she would never get a chance to know now that he'd been dead almost three years. She had always felt like a piece of her was missing. This was not something her mother had ever understand, nor had it seemed that she'd tried to.

"Hey, Holly. Are you coming to the Christmas party this weekend?" one of her co-workers called from the side of her cubicle.

Holly grimaced and then forced a half-smile to her face, "I'm not sure quite yet."

"Oh, come on. Everyone's going to be there. You just have to come."

"I'll see," she agreed noncommittally. The last thing she wanted to do was attend a festive holiday party where everyone was smiling and having fun. That just wasn't her this year. Not now.

She turned at her desk and looked at the small picture of her mother when she was much younger. She picked it up and gently ran her fingertip around the bronze frame, "Mom...I can't believe you're really gone. I wish I would have done things differently. I wish I could have been there for you...with you..."

She returned from covering a human-interest story five weeks earlier, to find her editor waiting for her. He'd received a phone call from a hospital, looking for Holly. It seemed her mother had suffered a heart attack and had not made it. Holly had been devastated. Her editor had been compassionate and driven her the thirty miles to the adjoining town so that she could sign the paperwork and see for herself that her mother had died.

Since the funeral, which was held two days later, Holly had been plagued by regrets. Her mother had been much too young to die, just barely turned forty, and it had been so sudden. She felt cheated and as if she'd wasted the last three years of her life, staying angry over a man she'd never met, who hadn't cared enough about her or her mother to stick around.

She'd found herself sitting silently for long periods of time, remembering her childhood and realizing how hard it had been on her mother to raise a young daughter on her own. Sarah had been even more handicapped than most eighteen-year-old new mothers because she'd been raised Amish. She'd never even left her Amish Ordnung, a word she'd heard her mother use several times, until she'd met and married Brian Sanders.

Holly wasn't aware of just how hard it had been on her mother to find herself living in the Englisch world, pregnant, and divorced. Sarah had hidden much of that from her daughter, but after her death, Holly had begun doing some research into the Amish lifestyle and had started to get a clearer picture of the hardships her mother would have faced.

Her mother had never tried to return to the community she was raised in and Holly assumed that when she chose an Englischer over her family, they'd shunned her. By marrying Brian, she'd forsaken her family and friends completely. Her mother had never talked about her childhood, and Holly had always assumed it was because it wasn't something her mother particularly wanted to remember or dwell upon. After going through her mother's belongings, the day after the funeral, she'd realized that her mother had just not been one to complain about things she didn't feel she could change.

"Woolgathering?" her editor asked, peering at her over the wall of her cubicle.

She straightened up and tried for a smile, but failed miserably. "Not really."

"Uh huh. I don't buy that for a minute."

Holly shrugged her shoulders and then asked, "Did you need something?"

"For you to smile again, but I'll settle for a human-interest piece."

"Okay," Holly nodded, "did you have something specific in mind?"

Her editor smiled and she narrowed her eyes, knowing that grin meant he was about to meddle and there wouldn't be anything she could do to stop it from happening. Not if she wanted to keep her job. "I think our readers would love to hear how different cultures celebrate the holidays."

"Cultures?" she asked suspiciously.

"Yes. You know, Jewish, Asian, Amish…"

At his mention of the word Amish she knew where this was heading, and strangely enough, she found she didn't even want to fight him on it. "And you want me to research…?"

"The Amish, since you've seemed so fascinated with their culture of late."

Holly knew he'd seen her looking up information on the Amish culture more than once over the last few weeks. He'd asked her about it, and she'd told him in confidence that her mother had been raised Amish but had never spoken much about it or even tried to go back to visit her family.

He'd nodded and the next morning, she'd found a list of websites sitting on her desk. Some of them were managed by former Amish themselves, and others were simply outsiders' observations. She'd found a wealth of information in those pages and had a growing desire to meet her mother's family and to see firsthand how they lived.

"I'll do it," she informed him before either of them could change their minds.

He looked at her, nodded once, and then strolled away, whistling a children's Christmas song. She stared after him for a moment and then called out, "I'm taking a field trip..."

"Take the entire week," he called back without turning around.

Holly smiled, for the first time in what seemed like weeks, actually looking forward to this assignment. She now had a perfect reason to visit the local Amish communities, and she knew which one she was going to focus her efforts on – the one located in Lawrence County. The place where her mother had been born and raised.

Beliefs and Differences

Two days later…

Holly drove into the small town of New Wilmington and used her phone GPS to locate the bed and breakfast she would be staying at during her time here. She'd spent the day before making these arrangements, and perusing through the small box of things her mother had kept over the years.

There had been very little in the way of things from her Amish past, but Holly hadn't lost faith. She had a name, and a place, and if her research into the Amish lifestyle was correct, her mother's family was probably still living in the same house, doing the same things as before.

She looked around her as she parked the car, amazed at how festive everything seemed. She'd discovered during her research that the Amish were not the only inhabitants of New Wilmington, and had managed to find a way to co-exist with their Englisch neighbors. According to some of the articles and websites she'd visited, the Amish maintained their lifestyle, and the Englisch who chose to live amongst them were very conservative and understanding . The B&B where she would be staying was one example of that relationship.

The owner was an older couple who were not Amish, but respected their neighbors' beliefs and did their best to made their differences as unnoticeable as possible. For instance, their website had advertised satellite television, and yet from the street, there was no evidence of a satellite dish to be seen. Holly appreciated the fact that these two cultures lived so close to one another and seemed to get along. Unfortunately, it also left her with more questions concerning why her mother had left here and never returned. She understood that her father was not part of the Amish community, but it seemed to her that they could have existed close by easy enough and for some reason had chosen not to. Something she hoped she could come to understand during the next week or so.

She slipped out of the car, locking the doors and then turned away from the B&B and headed down the main sidewalk. She pushed her hands into the pockets of her wool coat, glad she'd brought it along with her hat and gloves. A couple of inches of fresh snow had fallen during the previous night, and the Christmas lights scattered amongst some of the storefronts made it seem as if Christmas was right now. A gentle breeze blew the snow around her ankles, making her even more thankful for fur-lined winter boots.

She paused for a moment in front of an obviously Amish store that had a gorgeous quilt displayed in the window. She glanced at the small drugstore next door and immediately noticed the contrasts. A further inspection of other storefronts made it easy to spot the Amish ones from the other. Wreaths with large bows hung from the street lamps, garland was strung up around entryways, and the Amish stores had placed candles in the windows. Some of the Englisch stores had tastefully decorated Christmas trees displayed inside, but the Amish storefronts were simple and mostly unadorned. She'd read online that the Amish considered Christmas trees, lights, and the other commercial items of the holiday season to be pagan. Christmas was all about Christ and remembering the birth of a baby two thousand years earlier, not Rudolph, snowmen, or Santa.

She'd celebrated Christmas as a child, but now her mother's reticence and discomfort with the holiday made more sense. She'd done her best to give her daughter a normal childhood, but she'd been completely out of her depth and in unfamiliar territory. A pain of guilt and sadness swamped Holly for a moment. Mom had it so hard raising me in an unfamiliar place by herself, and towards the end, I was so ungrateful...I was a horrible daughter to her.

Two children rushed by her, pulling her from her somber thoughts and into the jubilant atmosphere of the small town. Everywhere she looked, she saw people milling about with large smiles upon their faces. She watched them as she walked along, wishing she had the right to join in their fun. A mixture of Amish and non-Amish walked along the sidewalk, with their children playing with one another in the fresh snow.

She found a vacant bench outside what appeared to be a local barbershop, and she took a seat and just watched the people strolling past. Several groups of Amish women and men walked past her, and she watched them with avid curiosity on her face. The more she'd researched them, the more she'd found herself intrigued by their simple way of life. She was determined to learn everything she could about them while staying here.

She longed for a connection to this people, and towards that end, she pulled a photograph she'd found of her mother when she much younger from her coat pocket. Her mother had been wearing a simple dress with her hair pinned back and secured atop her head, but the clothing wasn't Amish. She knew that because there were obviously buttons visible on her shirt. How exactly does one make a shirt and hide the buttons? Another question I would love to have answered.

A snowball landed by her feet and she looked up from the picture to see to chagrined children rushing towards her with looks of alarm on their faces. They spoke to her rapidly in a language she guessed was Pennsylvania Dutch, but didn't understand.

She smiled at them and shook her head, "I'm sorry, but I don't understand you."

"They were apologizing for being rude and including you in their snowball fight without your permission," a smooth voice came from her left side.

Holly turned her head and stared up into the gray eyes of a very handsome Amish man. His face showed he wasn't a green youth, and his unshaven face declared him unmarried. Why that thought made her pulse kick up, she wasn't quite sure, but the way he was looking at her brought her back to the fact that two red-faced little boys were standing in front of her awaiting her verdict.

She smiled at them, "That's okay. You didn't actually hit me with the snowball, and on another day I might actually join you, but not today."

The man standing to her left spoke to the boys and then nodded their heads and then scampered off. He then spoke to her, his accent strong, and his English nearly perfect, with only the occasional Amish word sprinkled in. "They are gut kinner."

"I'm sure they meant no harm," she agreed with a nod. She'd done her research, as any good journalist would, and had acquainted herself with some basic Amish words. She was now very glad she'd done that.

"You are visiting?" the young man inquired.

Holly nodded, "Yes, or should I say Jah?"

He grinned at her, "You speak our language?"

Holly smiled and shook her head, "Nee, I just taught myself a few words from the Internet."

He nodded his head, "The Internet. The Amish have no need of such devices. It is better to learn from doing." He looked up at a noise from down the street, "I must go. Enjoy your stay here."

Holly started to ask his name and introduce herself, but he was gone as quickly as he'd appeared. Shrugging, she stood up and headed towards the small quilt shop. Might as well begin asking questions and see where it gets me. She stepped inside and smiled as the owners came forward to greet her. She explained her reason for being there and how her mother had been raised Amish. She then showed then the picture and looked at them expectantly for some sign of recognition.

They looked at her picture, murmuring between themselves, and then directed her to another shop down the street where several members of long-standing Amish could be found. If anyone was able to help her, it would be them.

She thanked them and headed in that direction, hiding her disappointment that her first endeavor to find someone who had known her mother had failed. But she was a journalist at heart and loved solving a good mystery or riddle. Deciding to approach this task I that frame of mind, she hastened her steps and began her search in earnest.

It paid off, and the older woman manning the counter in the shop took the picture and nodded, "Jah. This is Sarah, is it not?"

Holly smiled for the first time in weeks and nodded, "My mother."

"I haven't seen your mamm for many years. Must be going on twenty now."

"Twenty-two to be exact. Do you know where I could find her family?"

"Her familye still manage one of the local dairy farms."

"A dairy farm?" she asked, never having given much thought to what her extended family might do for a living.

"Jah. If you want to meet some of your mamm's familye there is a farmer's market inside the livery tomorrow morning. Many of the Ordnung bring their goods to be sold during this time as the Englisch are frequent visitors. This close to Christmas, most everyone should be in attendance."

"Tomorrow? I can do that. Do you know what the name of their farm is?" Holly asked, feeling hope blossom inside her chest at the prospect of meeting some of her extended family.

"Just ask around, they will be found if that is their desire."

"But...," Holly began, confused because the shop owner had been so helpful up to this point.

"Your mamm left of her own accord and in doing so, she cut herself off from her familye.

It is for them to decide if they wish to know you, not mine."

Holly slowly nodded her head and then turned around and left the small shop. She didn't want to offend anyone, but just knowing that her mamm's familye was nearby sent a feeling or urgency through her. She was so close, and yet she had no control when it came to moving things forward. That would be up to them.

She headed towards the bed and breakfast, intending to get settled and hopefully do some more research into this particular Amish community before the morning arrived. She wanted to be as prepared as possible, should she be lucky enough to actually meet someone from her familye tomorrow.

Christmas Blessings

The next morning…

Holly stepped inside the barn and was momentarily transfixed by the number of Amish present. Wooden tables, carts laden with a variety of produce and preserved foods, colorful quilts, and wooden furniture was displayed in neat rows. The Amish themselves were a little hard to tell apart, all dressed in plain fabric dresses of royal blue, navy blue, black and varying shades of brown. The men wore dark denim trousers with a double placket on the front and suspenders to hold them up, and a traditional felt hat, while the women, except the very youngest children, all wore either white or black prayer kapps.

Holly smiled at her mental use of the Amish terms. Her research had intrigued her, and she'd challenged herself to use the German derivatives as often as possible while in New Wilmington.

She wandered down the aisles, looking at the various offerings and searching for anyone who might resemble her mamm or be from a dairy farm. She was concentrating so hard, she didn't realize she was also frowning until a familiar voice spoke above her head.

"We meet again."

Holly whirled around and looked up into the gray eyes of the mann she'd met the day before. "Oh, hello."

"Gutentag. You wish to buy something?"

Holly shook her head, "Not really, I was just wandering a bit."

The mann looked at her curiously and then shook his head, "I think you do not tell the whole truth. You seemed to be looking for something particular."

Holly was amazed and huffed out a short laugh, "You would be right. Are you a mind reader?"

He smiled and shook his head, "Nee, just observant." He looked over her shoulder for a moment and then returned his attention to her, "My name is Evan Miller."

Holly extended her hand, and then let it drop when he merely looked at it. Silly, Amish don't shake hands, especially between opposite sexes. She rubbed her palm on her thigh and then smiled, "I'm Holly Sanders. Do you live around here?"

"All of my life," he confirmed, once again looking over her shoulder. She opened her mouth to say something else and then stopped as he turned away from her.

"Excuse me for a moment."

She watched as he strolled across the aisle and retrieved the hand of a little girl. He squatted down so that he was eye-level with her and seemed to be talking to her solemnly, when she threw her little body against his own and he hugged her close. He soothed her for a moment and then picked her up, carrying her back to where Holly still stood waiting.

"I apologize. Holly, this is my niece, Becca Yoder. Becca, this nice lady is Holly."

Holly looked at the little girl and then smiled, "Hello Becca."

The little girl simply stared back at her with big brown eyes full of too much sorrow for one so young.

Evan murmured in the little girl's ear, but she shook her head and buried her face in his neck. "I'm sorry. Becca is…well, she's a bit shy."

Holly nodded, thinking he'd meant to say something more, but had held back because of the little girl. An older girl approached just then, "Evan, is it okay if I take Becca over to sit with the lambs?"

Evan looked for a response from his niece, but when none was forthcoming, he sighed and then set her down on the ground. "Becca, go with Miriam for a bit. I'll come get you in twenty minutes."

Becca took the other girl's hand and allowed herself to be led away, her expression never changing at all.

Evan watched after her, a look of helplessness on his face for a moment before he hid it. "Becca's had a rough time in recent months." He turned back to Holly, "Her mamm was my older schwestern. Ruth. She and her husband were killed in a house fire a few months and Becca came to live with me. She hasn't spoken a word since the fire."

Holly's heart broke for the little girl, "That's horrible."

"I have to believe it was Gott's will, but there are times when my faith is tested."

Holly looked at him in confusion, "You think Gott wanted her parents to die in a fire?"

Evan shook his head, "Nee, that is not what I meant or think at all. The Amish believe that Gott has a purpose for each of our lives. We are not to question it, but trust Him in all that we do. I don't why Ruth was taken from this earthly existence so soon, but I believe that we will be reunited one day in Heaven. Until that time, I will look after Becca to the best of my ability."

"That's a lot of responsibility," Holly told him, thinking about the information she'd discovered about her own mamm and how hard being a single parent had been.

Evan smiled, "This I know. But, enough about my troubles. What is Holly Sanders looking for?"

"Answers," she replied before she could think about her response. She looked up when she realized what she'd done, but Evan didn't seem too concerned with her response.

"Well, answers can be easy to obtain, but first one must know the question."

Holly nodded, and then blurted out, "My mamm was raised here."

"In Pennsylvania?" Evan asked.

Holly shook her head, "Right here in New Wilmington. She was Amish and left when she married an Englischer."

Evan's face closed down briefly and then he seemed to catch himself and he slowly asked, "What was your mamm's name?"

"Sarah Bontrager."

Evan was silent for a moment and then asked, "Is your mamm here with you?"

Holly shook her head, "She passed away a few months ago. I knew she was Amish, but she never wanted to talk about that period of her life. I was hoping to find some of her familye by coming here."

Evan looked off across the barn for a moment and then seemed to come to a decision. "I will help you do this."

"You will?" she asked, surprise in her voice.

"Jah. Everyone should know their familye. Your mamm made a decision to leave here, but that doesn't mean she became any less her parent's dochder. I personally do not like the way the elders of the past handled these types of situations, and while things have changed only a tiny bit in the past twenty years, kinner who choose to leave the Ordnung are not shunned the way they used to be. Unfortunately, you mamm was probably very aware that she would be cutoff entirely from her familye when she left."

Holly nodded, "I don't know much about that time of her life, but I was hoping to maybe find some friends or others who might have remembered her. I would really like to know more about my heritage."

"Heritage is a gut thing. I will make some inquiries on your behalf. Will you be staying in town?"

Holly gave him the name of the bed and breakfast where she was staying and he smiled, "They are very nice people and you will enjoy your stay there. I will send word to you there if I find anything out."

Holly bit her bottom lip, "Thank you. Why are you helping me?" He was a very good looking young man, and Holly acknowledged that she found him very attractive, even though he was Amish.

Evan smiled at her, "I'm helping you because I like you."

Holly raised a brow, "You like me?"

"Jah. I've never met anyone like you and would like to learn more about your world."

"What do you want to know?" she asked him, willing to tell him about her world if he was going to help her locate her familye.

Evan grinned at her, "We will have to save that conversation for a later date. I need to go retrieve Becca and get her home for her lunch. Holly, have a gut day and I will speak to you again soon."

Holly nodded and watched him stride away. She spent the rest of the morning wandering around the small town before returning to the bed and breakfast. The Marlow's owned the five bedroom haus and Mrs. Marlow was baking cookies when she returned.

"Come and join me, dear and tell me what you've been up to today."

Holly did so, helping cutout and then decorate sugar cookies in a variety of Christmas shapes and sizes. She told Mrs. Marlow about meeting Evan and his offer to help, at which Mrs. Marlow merely smiled and told her what a fine young man Evan Miller was. She was lucky to have met him and have him on her side. As she climbed the stairs to her assigned room several hours later, she found herself unable to stop thinking about the gray eye, dark wavy hair, and gentle nature of the mann.

The way he'd handled his niece's silence spoke volumes, and Holly was once again reminded that it was easy to tell the measure of a mann by how he treated small children and animals. Evan Miller was indeed a gut mann and Holly figured Becca was blessed to have him in her life.

The Boy Next Door

The next afternoon…

While Holly was waiting for Evan to contact her, she busied herself speaking with various members of the community, as well as helping Mrs. Marlow bake Christmas cookies and goodies for the annual Christmas Program the kinner would be putting on Christmas Eve night. The bed and breakfast had all of the traditional holiday adornments, including a large tree with sparkling lights and glass ornaments. Inside the small establishment, it was easy to forget where she was.

But outside and amongst the town, the differences were stark. Holly found herself intrigued with the simpler decorations she found in the Amish shops. Stars and evergreen wreaths with handmade bows and berries seemed to be the most common decorations. Nothing flashy, and nothing that wasn't completely handmade. No strings of lights, no Christmas trees…even the wrapping paper they used was plain and unadorned. It seemed the simple life extended to all facets of their existences.

Now that the days were shorter, they even used oil lanterns to light their small shops.

She went with Mrs. Marlow late afternoon the next day to deliver her contribution to the Christmas program, and was admiring the song the kinner were singing, when she noticed a young girl sitting all alone on a bench by the wall. She recognized her as being Becca Yoder, and looked around for her uncle. Not finding him, Holly made her way over to the little girl and sat down beside her.

"Hello, Becca. Do you remember me? We met in the barn yesterday. You were with your Uncle Evan?"

Becca looked up at her but refused to say anything. Holly tried again, "Is your uncle here?"

Becca gave a short shake of her head and then turned her attention back to the front of the building where the other kinner were practicing their poems and songs.

Holly was concerned and felt compassion for the little girl. She paused for a moment and then asked, "You don't like to sing? I bet you have a beautiful voice."

Becca ignored her and Holly thought maybe she was being ignored, when she noticed the little girl's fingers were keeping time with the music. She's heartbroken, but not lost. She probably loved to sing before...

Mrs. Marlow joined them and leaned down, giving the little girl a hug that wasn't returned. "Miss Becca, how are you today?" She paused while she waited for a response and then carried on as if one had been given, "Well, I'm doing fine as well."

Holly watched the interaction, making a mental note to ask Mrs. Marlow about the little girl's silence when they were alone. "Is someone watching her?" she asked instead.

"The kinner are all practicing for the Christmas program. I'm sure her teacher is around here somewhere. They'll head back to their homes anytime now."

Holly nodded and then stood up, "I didn't want to just leave her sitting here if she were lost or something of that sort."

"She's not lost, she's just grieving," Mrs. Marlow told her quietly. "Becca, tell your uncle hello from me and to bring you to dinner one day this week." She looked at Holly and gestured towards the doors, "She'll be fine."

Holly was torn, but then again, the little girl was not her responsibility. She followed Mrs. Marlow back to her vehicle, relaxing when she spied Evan driving a buggy into the parking area. "Looks like Evan just arrived to pick her up."

Mrs. Marlow smiled, "Evan is doing a remarkable job. It's not every day a young mann of twenty-six takes on the responsibility of raising his five-year-old niece. He never even got to grieve the loss of his schwestern."

"It must be hard on them both. Does he not have anyone to help?" She didn't want to think of Evan having a wife, and tried to tell herself that wasn't why she'd asked the question.

Mrs. Marlow shook her head, "His parents were older and died some years back. He works the land that has been in his familye's possession for decades before."

"Evan's a farmer?" Holly asked, soaking up the information she was being given and trying to reconcile the Evan she'd barely begun to know with the one Mrs. Marlow was describing.

"Evan's parents were already in their late fifties when he and his schwestern came along. They both died a few years back, a few months apart from one another. And then the house fire happened and Evan's schwestern was taken away as well. He was never around kinner while growing up and

I've been amazed at how well he's adjusted to having young Becca living with him."

"He mentioned that she hasn't talked since the accident?" Holly asked, becoming even more interested in learning about Evan Miller. He had those boy-next-door good looks that so many of her friends growing up had oohed and aahed over. The fact that he'd put his own plans aside and taken in his niece was amazing. She knew and worked with a number of single young men in their latter twenties, and she couldn't imagine any of them putting aside their own plans to care for a little girl.

"Becca was trapped by the fire and a neighbor managed to get her out before the smoke got to her. They didn't live here, but about an hour's drive south. Evan was contacted through the local police and went down to deal with things. We were all surprised when he returned with Becca."

"She must have been so scared," Holly murmured, trying to imagine what the little girl had suffered while waiting to be rescued.

Mrs. Marlow nodded her head, "I cannot imagine. I'm sure the trauma is what has made her go silent. Bishop Miller believes she will speak again once her mind has a chance to heal."

"I hope so, she's a beautiful little girl."

Mrs. Marlow smiled, "But in the Amish world beauty is vanity and to be avoided lest it corrupts the soul."

"You sound very knowledgeable about all things Amish," Holly commented.

Mrs. Marlow nodded, "That's because I was raised around the Amish most of my life. They are a simple people and mostly misunderstood by those in the outside world. Englisch is what they call outsiders, whether they are actually of English descent or not."

"I read that online. It seems like it would be very hard to leave here and adjust to the place where I live. I just keep wondering why my mamm would have done such a thing."

"Many people, even Amish youngster, think the grass is greener on the other side. They are tempted by what they don't have, and sometimes it gets the better of them. In your mamm's case, I imagine she was struggling with rebellion and an Englischer who thought he was doing her some big favor by taking her away from everything she knew."

Holly considered that for a moment, "My parents didn't stay married very long. According to her, my daed was a drunkard and abusive. I don't think she realized his true nature until they were already married.

She only stayed with him for a few months and left because of me."

Mrs. Marlow was quiet for a moment and then suggested, "When Evan finds your familye, keep an open mind. Things might not be as you assume."

Holly started to ask for an explanation, but they had arrived back at the bed and breakfast and Mrs. Marlow was already out of the vehicle and heading for the kitchen door. "Well, I'm not sure what she meant by that, but keep an open mind I most certainly will do."

Realizing she was talking to herself out loud, she exited the vehicle and headed for her assigned room. She'd do a bit more research on the Amish and their lifestyle, in the hopes that one day soon she would be able to meet some of her mamm's familye and not embarrass herself in the process of getting to know them. She wanted to fit in so badly, and just the prospect of knowing she had relatives that were alive put a smile upon her face. Maybe I'm not all alone in this world after all.

Being Amish

Three days later...

"Holly, Evan and Becca are coming to dinner this evening. I was wondering if you would mind helping me in the kitchen?" Mrs. Marlow asked her as she sipped her first cup of tea a few days later.

"I would be happy to, but I have to confess, I do better with a microwave than a stove top."

Mrs. Marlow chuckled, "You'll do fine. I'll talk you through everything. I'm surprised that your mamm didn't teach you how to cook, being Amish and all."

Holly shook her head, "She worked all the time. I didn't realize how hard things must have been for her once she left my daed. She was a waitress at an all-night diner, and I can remember she often worked the evening shift because the tips were better.

"She would pick me up from school and I would spend the evening in the backroom watching the small television there and doing my homework. She would check on me often, and I grew up thinking it was normal to spend so much time away from one's apartment."

Holly sighed and made a face, "I never realized the sacrifices she made for me until it was too late. I was in high school before I realized started to want what other kids had. I thought that if I could just find my daed maybe things would be all right and she wouldn't have to work so much."

Mrs. Marlow joined her at the table, "Did you ever find him?"

Holly nodded, "In the pages of the obituaries. He passed away not too long before I went looking for him. I blamed her, of course. I thought I could save him, but I've since come to realize he didn't want to be saved. He lived life on the streets by choice."

"That must have been hard to discover."

"A little. It was harder when I found out she'd died from a heart attack and I hadn't had the chance to tell her I was sorry for putting all of the blame on her. I still regret that."

Mrs. Marlow made a tsking sound and then stood up, "Regrets steal the future. Come into the kitchen and I will show you how to make bread. That is sure to get your mind thinking about other things."

"Bread?"

Mrs. Marlow looked at her and then laughed, "Bread. Trust me, every woman should know how to make a decent loaf of bread."

Holly followed her with a smile, "I did tell you I can't cook, right?"

"Oh ye of little faith. Everyone can cook with a little help."

*****

Seven hours later…

Holly heard the front doors open and she had to make herself slow down as she headed for the first floor. Evan was taking Becca's woolen coat off just as she reached the bottom of the staircase, and he looked up at her and smiled warmly.

"Gutennacht Holly. Something smells amazing."

"That would be the bread that Holly made earlier today."

Evan grinned at Mrs. Marlow and then smiled at Holly, "You made bread?"

Holly blushed and nodded, "Mrs. Marlow decided I needed to learn how to cook."

"Cooking is a gut thing and Mrs. Marlow does it well. Learning from her is also a gut thing."

Holly smiled and then addressed Becca, "How are you?" Becca didn't respond, but then Holly was prepared for that. "Do you want to come sit with me while dinner finishes cooking? I found some coloring books and crayons in a drawer upstairs. I thought maybe you could help me color a picture."

Becca looked at her shyly for a moment, and then directed her eyes back towards the ground. "Holly, I'm sorry…"

"Don't be," she assured Evan with a shake of her head. She walked over and extended her hand to the little girl, "Come on, Becca. We'll let Uncle Evan keep Mrs. Marlow entertained. Mr. Marlow is out back cutting some more firewood."

Holly held her breath until the little girl slowly put her fingers in Holly's hand. She nodded once and then walked the little girl down the hallway to where a coloring book and box of crayons sat on the wooden table.

Holly helped her get seated on the high chair and then she opened the book and began slowly turning the pages. "You tell me when you want me to stop. You can color the right page and I'll color the left one."

Becca made no comment, but when Holly was about halfway through the book, her little hand suddenly came off her lap and landed on a page with two kittens playing with a ball of yarn on one side, and a cat cleaning her paw on the other.

"Oh, you like kittens?" Holly asked. She waited for Becca to respond, pleased when the little girl nodded once. "I've never had a kitten." She kept up a small conversation about cats and kittens while she opened the box of crayons and spilled them across the table. Becca picked up a black one and began coloring one of the kittens.

Holly watched her from the corner of her eye and thought things were going well until she saw the first teardrop hit the coloring book. She looked over to see tears flowing down Becca's face, her mouth turned down in sorrow as she silently cried.

"Oh, sweetie! I didn't intend to make you cry," Holly put down the crayon and pulled the little girl unresisting onto her lap. She wrapped her arms around her and rocked back and forth, "It's okay. I know things seem bad right now, but Uncle Evan loves you."

"I miss Smokey," a teeny tine voice mumbled against her neck.

Holly's breath stalled even as her heart shouted for joy. She talked! "Who is Smokey, sweetie?"

"My kitten. He burned up like..." The gravity of what she'd been just about to say stopped her words as fresh tears assailed her. This time, not so quietly. Holly sensed Evan's presence before she saw him step into the room.

His eyes took in the scene before him and he mouthed, "What happened?"

Holly felt her own tears spill over as she held the sobbing little girl in her arms, "We were coloring kittens and she started crying. She misses Smokey."

Knowing entered Evan's eyes and his shoulders sagged, "Her kitten."

"Jah," Holly answered him, the use of the Amish term falling from her lips so easily.

Evan gave her a smile and came and sat down behind them, placing a tender hand on his niece's head, "Becca, do you miss your kitten?"

Becca's sobs had lessened some, and she nodded her head, but refused to talk to her uncle, even though he tried multiple times. Finally, after ten minutes or so, he stood up, "I'll let you two finish what you were doing. Dinner's almost ready, Mrs. Marlow asked me to inform you."

"Evan...," Holly called to him, not knowing what to do to correct what she saw as a problem. His niece, who hadn't spoken a word to him since the fire, had talked to her, but wouldn't talk to him.

Evan smiled at her tenderly and shook his head, "Don't apologize. I am so grateful that she has chosen to speak again, I don't care if it is not to me yet. Danke, Holly. You are an answer to my prayers."

Holly shook her head, "I'm not anyone's answer to prayer."

Evan stepped back towards her and squatted down so that they were on eye-level, "You are mine. Danke."

After he left the room, Holly spent a few minutes picking up the spilled crayons while Becca quietly told her about the ten-week old kitten that had perished in the fire along with her parents. Holly knew that kinner didn't process death in the same way as adults, and it seemed that she was accepting of the fact that her mamm and daed were now in Heaven with Gott, but was heartbroken over the loss of her pet.

Several hours later, Becca had fallen asleep on the couch, the unfinished picture of the kittens held tightly in her hands. Holly looked at her and then realized that Evan was watching her from across the room.

"Would you care to take a short walk with me?" he asked.

"Sure," Holly nodded, "Just let me grab a coat. It's chilly outside."

"Jah. More snow is expected tomorrow and the next day."

They walked around the gardens in the back of the bed and breakfast, a high moon lighting their path. "I'm really sorry that Becca won't talk to you," she began again.

Evan stopped and turned her to face him, his hands resting gently on her shoulders, "Please don't apologize. She's talking and crying. Do you know, she hasn't cried once?"

Holly nodded, "She told me without any sadness that her parents were with Gott, but she cried over the kitten. Is there any possible way she could have another kitten?" She realized how she might sound and backtracked, "Sorry, I know that's not my place to even suggest..."

"Nee. Stop apologizing for caring. I'm know sure if anyone has kittens at this time of year. Most of the kittens are born to barn cats and must be taken and tamed as soon as they are weaned to make good house pets."

"Well, maybe in the Spring she could get another one?"

"Jah, maybe in the Spring."

Holly looked at the sleeping girl and silently wished there was a way to replace her kitten now, but it was December, and if barn cats were the only source of kittens in the area,

Spring was probably the only option available. Maybe there's something else she could love just as well?

"I should take her back to the haus, but first I wanted to let you know I was able to track down your mamm's parents and some of her school friends."

Holly smiled broadly, "Really? Her parents are still alive?"

"Jah. They own a dairy farm in a neighboring Ordnung. I spoke to the new bishop yesterday and he think they would welcome a visit from you."

Holly's wish seemed like it was going to come true, and she had Evan to thank for it. Before she could think about the inappropriateness of her gesture, she threw her arms around him and hugged him, "Thank you. Danke. However else you want me to say it."

Evan held himself rigidly for a long moment, and just as she realized that what she'd done wasn't acceptable in his culture, his body relaxed and his arms came around her back and he hugged her in return. His voice was a bit scratchy and soft when he murmured above her head, "You are very welcome. I cannot drive you there tomorrow, but I could do so the day after. If that is acceptable?"

Holly pulled herself away from him, feeling the heat stain her cheeks when she realized just how safe and right it had felt to be in his arms. He's Amish and they don't hug like that. He probably only hugged you back because he didn't know what else to do.

"I...the day after tomorrow?...you will drive me there?"

"Well, in my buggy, Jah. I will drive you there. Becca will need to tag along."

"That won't be any problem." In fact, having the little girl along will help keep my wandering thoughts about how handsome you are at bay.

"Gut! I will come by for you around 8 o'clock."

"In the morning?" she asked, dismay in her voice and showing on her face.

Evan chuckled, "Jah, in the morning. The sun will be up around 6 and I should be done with the morning chores by 7. I will be here at 8 o'clock."

Morning chores? Holly nodded her head, "Fine. I'll be ready to go."

Evan gave her a smile and then picked up Becca, smiling down on her sleeping form when she rolled into his body and wrapped a small arm around his neck. "Danke once again."

Holly blushed and nodded her head silently. Evan gave her one more glance and then headed for the front door. Mr. Marlow was just coming back inside with an armful of wood for the fireplaces and held the door open for him. "Goodnight, Evan."

"Gutennacht, Mr. Marlow. Dinner was very good, as always."

"We enjoyed having you and getting to see Becca. Drive safe."

"We will. Holly, I will see you the day after tomorrow. Sleep well."

A Day Blessed by Gott

Two days later...

Holly was nervous. Evan had picked her up half an hour ago, and Becca had offered her the tiniest of smiles, but no words. They were currently driving down the small street of the neighboring town where her grandparents lived. Evan had suggested they stop at a local bakery for some breakfast before getting directions to the dairy farm where her mamm had grown up.

He parked the buggy next to several others that looked just alike, only their horses were different. "Let me help you down," he told her, coming around and holding onto her elbow as she stepped from the buggy. Becca followed her out and then reached for her hand.

Holly took it and smiled down in to her face, "Are you hungry?" Becca nodded, but once again, remained verbally silent. "So am I."

Evan escorted them to the door, and as Holly and Becca stepped inside, they were assailed by the smell of butter and sugar, and the clanging of the bell overhead. Wooden floors creaked as they walked towards the small counter, and Holly inhaled deeply the smell of fresh pastries and hot coffee. "It smells delicious."

"Welcome, what can I get for you today?" a middle-aged woman behind the counter asked in broken English.

"I'm going to have one of those cinnamon twists," Holly told her and then she squatted down next to Becca. "What kind of pastry do you like to eat, sweetie?"

Becca was eyeing the various offerings and eventually pointed to a cake donut covered in colored sprinkles. Holly smiled and nodded, "That is a gut choice." She told the clerk Becca's choice and then watched as Evan made his selection, also ordering a glass of milk for his niece and two cups of kaffe for himself and her.

"We're going to find a place to sit down. Is my grandparent's place far from here?"

Evan looked at her and then shook his head, "I don't really know, but I'll ask." He turned back to the clerk, "Excuse me, but do you happen to know where the Bontrager dairy farm is located?"

The clerk eyed them both suspiciously and asked, "Are they expecting you?"

Evan shook his head, "Nee, but this is a surprise I think they will like." He gestured towards Holly, "This is their grossdochdern."

"What?! Who was your mamm?" the clerk asked, coming around the counter in haste.

Holly met the woman's eyes, "Sarah Bontrager."

"Oh my!" She looked Holly up and down and then hugged her tightly, "Welcome, Holly. You look like your mamm when she was much younger. How is she? Is she with you?"

Holly stepped back and shook her head, "Nee. She died a few months ago."

The woman's eyes filled with tears, "Oh, I would have so liked to have talked with her again. But I'm forgetting my manners. My name is Dawn and your mamm and I were best friends until she left here." She called into the back of the bakery, "Anna! Abby! Sarah's dochdern is here."

"Sarah Bontrager?" another middle-aged woman asked, coming from the kitchen area with an apron and her hands covered in flour.

"Jah! Come and meet her," Dawn urged them both.

Holly found herself surrounded by voices all of a sudden, and it wasn't until a tiny hand pushed its way into her own that she remembered Evan and Becca were with her. "Sweetie, let's get you settled. Excuse me, but Becca needs to sit down and eat. Maybe you could talk with us while she does that?"

Dawn nodded and grabbed a tray and their selected items. Abby and Anna shook their heads, "We have work to do. Please come and see us again. We would love to know what your mamm did after leaving here."

Dawn returned and after Becca was settled, she pulled up another chair, "Is this your dochdern?"

Holly shook her head, part of her wishing for the first time in her adult life that she could say Becca was hers. She'd not really given the thought of having children much thought, but being around Becca, and getting to know Evan had changed that.

"Nee, she is Evan's niece. He is raising her in the absence of her parents who are in Heaven now." She spoke the words softly, not wanting to upset the little girl needlessly.

Dawn looked at Evan and then smiled, "That is well done of you. So, your familye is going to be so surprised."

Holly nodded, "I hope it will be a gut one."

"It will be. They were upset when she decided to live amongst the Englisch, but Brian would have never fit in here. He held everything that was Amish in great disdain and often told your mamm how idiotic he found our lifestyle. He called it bizarre and controlling."

"You met my daed?" Holly asked.

Dawn nodded her head, "I have to confess I never like him. After Ruth left here, I snuck away a few times and called her on the phone number she'd given me. She sounded terribly unhappy. Brian wasn't the man she thought he was, but she'd already left and the bishop at the time was a very hard mann who would have never allowed her back without making her grovel and embarrassing her. Ruth didn't deserve to be treated like that, so she made the decision to live in the Englisch world.

"It was very hard for her, and I wish we could have kept in touch, but the bishop discovered my actions and my parents forbid me from contacting her again."

Holly nodded, "She would have liked to have kept in contact with you, even though she never talked about her childhood."

"It was probably too painful. She gave up everything for you."

"For me?" Holly asked.

"Jah. She left Brian when she found out she was pregnant with you and he demanded she get an abortion."

Holly gasped, "She never told me that."

Dawn gave her a sad smile, "She wouldn't have, it was not her way. She suffered and endured many hardships, but she did it out of love for you."

Holly felt tears sting her eyes and then noticed that Becca and Evan were both finished and waiting for her, "My friends are done and I shouldn't keep them waiting any longer. Evan brought me here to meet my grandparents."

Dawn grinned, "Then I will come with you as well. I cannot wait to see the looks upon their faces. Oh, and you have a whole bunch of aunts and uncles, and cousins, and nieces and nephews...the Bontrager family is very large."

"My mamm had siblings?" Holly asked, the idea shocking her.

Dawn smiled, "She had seven brudern and schweschdern, all of which have their own familye now. Are you ready for such a big reunion?"

"Oh," she nodded eagerly, "Jah. Bitte."

"I can see you're already trying to fit in. Where are you staying?"

Holly told her about the bed and breakfast and the Dawn shook her head, "Nee, you should stay with me. I have an extra bedroom that is not being used and you will be close enough to walk over and visit your familye anytime you want."

"Really?" she asked, but then she looked at Evan and realized that if she stayed with Dawn, she might not see Evan again. "Can I think about that and get back to you?"

"Of course. Let me tell the others I'm leaving for a bit and I will lead the way with my own buggy. This is truly a day blessed by Gott."

The Perfect Day

Her first meeting with her grandparents was more than she could have ever hoped for. They welcomed her with open arms, and word spread quickly amongst the neighbors, and before midday had passed, she'd been introduced to so many people, she knew she'd never be able to remember all of their names.

Evan and Becca had been welcomed just as warmly, but when the other kinner had urged Becca to go play with them, she'd sidled up next to Holly and refused to leave her or Evan's side. By 3 o'clock, Becca was sleeping against Evan's shoulder and Holly knew it was time for her to leave.

"I cannot thank you enough for welcoming me so warmly. I wish I'd been able to meet you all sooner."

"No regrets, Holly. Your mamm did what she thought was best, and at the time, the only option really available to her was to leave our Ordnung and make her way in the Englisch world. Danke for coming to find us. After all of these years, Gott has finally heard our prayers and answered them."

Evan smiled and then whispered to her, "See, you're someone else's answer to prayer."

Holly blushed and then hugged her newfound familye, with promises to return soon. She was still mulling over Dawn's invitation to stay with her, and her grandparents had offered her the use of her mamm's old bedroom as well. She decided she wasn't going to make any decisions today, but wanted to sleep on things and then choose the best path.

She remained silent as they headed back to New Wilmington and the B&B, with Becca curled up on her side asleep, her head in Holly's lap. "She's very tired."

"She's had an exciting few days. Did you speak to you again today?"

Holly shook her head, "Nee, but things were very chaotic with so many new people to meet...I was overwhelmed at times today, I can only imagine how it must have been for her. Danke for bringing me here today. I never dreamed things would go this well."

"You are very welcome. I prayed that Gott would help prepare their hearts for your arrival."

"You do that a lot? Pray?"

"Jah. Do you never pray?" he asked in the gathering darkness.

Holly was quiet for long moments, "Not as much as I should. My mamm read her Bible a lot and prayed. We went to a small church, but she was always very quiet and didn't really want to get too involved in things."

"I imagine an Englisch church was much different than an Amish service. Here, we gather at the homes of our neighbors every few weeks. There are no musical instruments, and the sermons can last three or four hours. They are also always delivered in German."

"Three hours?"

"Jah. Things are very different here."

"I can see that. Did I miss something during lun

Evan smiled and then shook his head, "Nee, you did not. It is not our custom to have the genders intermingle at our gatherings. Not even married couples sit together when in mixed company. Now, in the privacy of their own haus, that is permissible."

"I thought maybe I had done something wrong. What if Becca would have insisted on staying with you?"

Evan pulled a face and then shook his head, "She would have been urged to sit with the other kinner or you. She would not have been welcome at the menner table."

"That seems so backward. In the Englisch world, boys and girls go out of their way to attract one another's attention. Here, you all try to avoid any interaction with the other sex."

"There is a reason for that."

Holly nodded and then addressed the impromptu hug she'd given him two nights earlier, "I'm sorry if my hug made you uncomfortable."

Evan was quiet for a moment, "While it is true that unmarried Amish women do not hug unmarried menner, your hug was…"

He stopped, as if at a loss for words. She gave him a moment, but when he didn't start speaking again, she tried to fill in the blank for him. "My hug was awful?"

Evan shook his head, "Nee. It was nice."

Holly felt her heartbeat speed up. Was it possible that Evan was as attracted to her as she was to him? That would be nice, but then again, he was Amish. How would that work exactly?

"So, you weren't offended?"

"Nee."

She decided to test the waters, "So if I was to do it again, you would…?"

Evan glanced at her and then sighed, "It would depend. If there was a reason for the hug, I would probably return it. Unless the bishop was somewhere near, and then we would both receive a stern lecture. That is something I would like to avoid at all costs."

"The bishop would lecture you?" Holly asked, teasing him just a bit.

"Jah. That is worse than when my daed would lecture my schweschdern and I."

"I'll try to contain my hugs to when no one else is around," she teased him, realizing that she was already looking forward to the next time she had a proper excuse to hug him. In the Amish world, that time probably didn't exist, but in this instance, she decided she could borrow some of her Englischer upbringing.

"So, what did you think about Dawn's offer of staying with her?" Evan asked in the quiet of the buggy.

"I really enjoyed talking with her, but I'm not sure I want to go stay with her. It didn't take us too long to travel here, and I'm very comfortable with the Marlow's right now. Besides, I owe my editor a story in the next few days about the differences between what I think of as Christmas and how the Amish celebrate the holiday."

"You are a writer?"

"A journalist for a newspaper. My editor knew I was interested in learning more about my mamm's familye and I personally think he came up with this assignment to give me an excuse to visit here."

"That would be very nice of him," Evan murmured. "Do you have enough information to write your article?"

"I do. Mrs. Marlow and some of the shopkeepers were very helpful. I've actually enjoyed getting to know some of them and realizing that by taking the commercialism out of Christmas, one can more easily remember the reason for the holiday."

"Without the birth of Christ, there is no Christmas," Evan concluded for her.

"Exactly. Back in Philadelphia, the department stores begin decorating for Christmas before Halloween, and it seems that everything is about Santa, reindeer, and presents. It was refreshing to hear some of the shopkeepers kinner explain the true meaning of Christmas and to hear them talk about how much fun they have playing board games with their friends and familye. I wish more kinner could experience that."

"You sound like you enjoy being here."

Holly nodded, "You sound surprised?"

"I am, honestly. Learning to live without all of the modern conveniences the Englisch world has to offer has got to be hard."

"How do you know about the modern conveniences?" she asked.

"I spent a few months during Rumspringa living amongst the Englisch and I made the decision to come back here. Life is so much simpler here and there is plenty of time to enjoy the little things in life. In the city, the little things became unnoticeable and that saddened me."

Holly knew exactly what he meant and nodded her head, "It seems that there is a lot less stress with your way of life."

"Stress is bad for the mind and the body. Do you plan to still be here at Christmas?" he asked as he pulled into the driveway of the B&B.

"I don't know. I don't really have anyone to spend it with back home."

"Would you consider having Christmas dinner with Becca and I?" Evan asked. "Mrs. Marlow has promised to cook the turkey, and several neighbors will be joining us as well. I'm sure if Becca were awake and in a speaking mood she would want you to stay. It's only another eight days away."

Holly looked at the sleeping girl and was certain she didn't want to spend Christmas anywhere else. "I think that would be lovely. What do you think Becca would like for Christmas?"

"The Amish don't do gifts like the Englisch do. Our gifts are more often than not practical in nature and very basic. Wooden toys, a new doll that has been handmade, a new kitchen tool or something for the barn. What did you have in mind?"

Holly smiled, "A kitten? Mrs. Marlow said one of the delivery men in town mentioned their house cat recently had a litter of kittens. One of them is all black with white mittens on its feet."

"That sounds like the picture she was coloring."

"I thought the same thing. Would it be okay with you if I obtained the kitten for her?"

Evan reached across the buggy and touched her cheek gently, "I can't think of anything she would like more. Again, I must give you thanks."

"I just want to see her smile," Holly told him. "If it makes her happy and gives her something to smile about, it will be the best present I've ever received."

"I look forward to seeing smiles upon both of your faces then."

Holly slid Becca off of her lap and then smiled at Evan, "Don't get out. Danke for today. I cannot tell you how much meeting my familye meant."

"I can see it in your eyes. Gutennacht Holly. But your thanks should be given to Gott, I was just an instrument to be used today. I will see you in a few days' time."

Holly slipped from the buggy and watched as he drove away. Instead of going straight into the house, she wandered around the side to the porch swing hanging there. She sat down and then looked up at the sky, "Gott, I don't know if you remember me or not...it's been so long since I last talked to you. I just wanted to say thank you for letting me come here and sending Evan and Dawn to help me meet my grandparents. I don't know what's happening to me, but I really like being here. Around these people. Living this simple lifestyle. I can't imagine going back to the real world."

She paused for a moment and then added, "I can't imagine never seeing Evan or Becca again. Gott, I've never been in love, and I'm not really sure this is even heading in that direction, but Evan is such a special person. So strong and dedicated to Becca and doing what is right, even if that means he has to put aside his own desires.

"When I hugged him, and then he hugged me back, I never wanted to leave his arms. It felt so safe there, something I haven't even truly felt. I guess I was hoping I would find that security when I met my daed, but then I felt even more alone."

"I probably don't have any right to ask this, but could you please help me figure what to do about these feelings I'm developing for Evan and Becca. I don't want to get my heart broken, and I don't want to see either of them hurt, but I'm falling for him. Show me which direction is right."

She finished her softly spoken prayer and looked up to see Mrs. Marlow standing on the patio. "That was a lovely prayer, dear. Be encouraged that Gott always hears our prayers. He might not answer in the way we would like, but He always hears us. Trust Him and everything will work out just fine."

Holly stood up, "I'm going to do my best. I met my grandparents and familye today and they were so loving and welcoming...I can't wait to go back and visit again."

"I'm happy for you, Holly. Did you and Evan have a gut time as well?"

"We did, but Becca was quiet all day long."

"She'll come around. She trusts you and that is a big step for her. Be patient and she'll start talking again soon."

Holly nodded her head and then took a cleansing breath of the brisk air, "Evan said the storm was going to hit during the night."

Mrs. Marlow smiled, "There will be a fresh blanket of snow come morning. How about a cup of hot cocoa before you go to bed?"

"That sounds like just what I need." Holly followed her hostess inside the kitchen. It was the perfect ending to a perfect day.

A Very Happy Christmas

Christmas morning…

Holly held the basket close to her chest, keeping the blanket Mrs. Marlow had loaned her over the top so that the bitter wind didn't chill what was inside. It was still fairly early, and she only hoped Becca wasn't yet out of bed and that she could be there when she came down the stairs.

Mr. Marlow had driven her over to Evan's house a few minutes earlier, promising to return with Mrs. Marlow and Christmas dinner in a few hours' time. Holly had thanked him kindly and headed towards the back door.

Evan was sitting at the table sipping his first cup of kaffe when she tapped gently on the window pane. He immediately opened the door and ushered her inside, "Becca just woke up and is getting dressed. You're just in time."

"Gut. I was hoping to get here before she came down for breakfast." A sound from inside the basket indicated the gift was getting anxious.

"Sounds like someone is ready to get out," Evan chuckled softly. "Oh, here she comes now. The second stair from the bottom creaks."

Becca wandered into the kitchen, saw Holly, and froze. "Becca, come say hello to Holly. She came to see you."

Becca looked between her uncle and Holly and then eyed the basket sitting on the table. Her eyes widened when a plaintive mewling sound came from beneath the blanket. She edged towards the table and leaned against Holly's side, "Kitty?"

The whispered words were like angelic music to both adults' ears. Holly swallowed back tears and nodded, "Open it and find out." Becca climbed up onto the bench and carefully pulled back the blanket to reveal the black kitten with green eyes and white socks on all four feet. "Kitty!"

Becca gingerly picked up the kitten and cradled her to her neck, whispering to the animal as it closed its eyes and purred loudly.

Holly felt tears spill over her cheeks and looked at Evan to see him having the same response. "Do you like your gift, Becca?"

She smiled and nodded, "Uncle Evan, is he mine?"

Evan nodded and cleared his throat several times before he could speak again, "Yes,

Becca. The kitten is yours. Holly gave him to you."

Becca leaned over and gave Holly a big kiss upon the cheek, "I love you Holly."

Holly wrapped her arms around the little girl and the kitten and kissed the top of her head, "I love you too, sweetie. Merry Christmas."

Epilogue

Three months later...

"Holly, Uncle Evan is here," Becca called from the front porch of the Bontrager haus. Holly had returned to Philadelphia shortly after the first of the year, and within a week had known that she no longer belonged in the Englisch world. She missed the simplicity of hand washing dishes and reading by firelight or lantern. She missed the quiet of the evenings and how many stars were up in the sky when the bright lights of the city were absent.

She missed Evan and Becca. And they missed her.

The day after Christmas, Evan had driven her to see her grandparents and a large dinner had been put together and for the next three days relatives had come from all over to make her acquaintance. Evan and Becca had only stayed for a few hours, and Evan had promised to return three days later to retrieve her.

She loved getting to know her familye and after returning to Philadelphia, she'd realized she was too far away to see them very often.

They didn't use phones and her only means for communicating with them was by letter since they didn't use electricity, so no computers or cell phones.

After going without a familye for so long, she was loathed to let her newfound one go so easily. Her editor and she talked it over, and he agreed to give her a part-time job where she could submit articles about the Amish lifestyle to the newspaper once a week.

She'd discussed the fact that she would have to send them in handwritten, and he'd balked at first and then capitulated, provided her handwriting was legible. Holly had smiled and promised him her penmanship was excellent.

She didn't have much in the way of material items since most of the furniture in her apartment was from a local rent to own stores. They were more than happy to take their merchandise back, with a substantial penalty, of course. She emptied her bank account, cancelled her credit cards, and sold her car.

A week after returning to Philadelphia, and she'd been ready to return to New Wilmington. She'd spoken with Mrs. Marlow, who had offered her a room for as long as she wanted it. She planned to ask her grandparents about staying with them for a few weeks, and they'd been thrilled at the prospect of getting to know her better.

Three months later, and she had finally come a decision about the future direction of her life. She'd been learning all about the Amish faith and Gott, and after spending time talking with the bishop and her familye, she'd decided to join the Amish faith. It wasn't a quick process, but Holly was up to the task.

She enjoyed learning everything, and most of all, she enjoyed getting to spend time with her familye and new friends. Evan's farm was only a few miles away, and he made time to visit her at least once a week on the pretense of Becca spending time with Holly.

Today, Evan had brought Becca over and then disappeared with one of Holly's uncles. Holly could tell he was planning something, but when he stepped into the haus and sent Becca outside for a moment, she knew her life was about to change.

"Holly, I know it's only been a few months, and I'm willing to wait a while if that is what you want, but I'm falling in love with you. Becca's been there for a long time, but I wanted you to know that I intend to formally court you from this day forward, with the hopes that one day soon, maybe even this summer, you'll marry me."

Holly was stunned and elated. "Jah, I will let you court me, and I'll even marry you when the time comes, but I want to be baptized into your Ordnung first."

Evan grinned from ear to ear at her and then whispered, "This would be a good time to exercise your right to hug me. The bishop is anywhere to be seen and we're all alone."

Holly didn't need any more prodding and threw herself into his waiting arms. She hugged him tight and then closed her eyes, "Danke, Gott."

Evan squeezed her in response to her whispered words, "What are you thanking Him for?"

"For you. For Becca. For bringing me here and letting me have this chance at happiness."

Evan hugged her tight and then set her away from him. It is not necessary to tell most people, but I think in this instance your familye would appreciate hearing about our plans."

Holly nodded and held his hand as they stepped from the haus to find most of her familye gathered in the yard. "Did they know this was going to happen?"

Evan shrugged, "I might have said something the other night."

Holly grinned, "Well, no matter. I can't wait to tell Becca. I bet she wants to bring the cat to the ceremony."

Evan shook his head, "That is not going to happen. The cat stays at the haus."

*****

Four months later...

Holly and Evan exchanged their vows, becoming husband and wife in the eyes of Gott and their familye and friends. Becca stood slightly behind them, a white wicker basket held in her hands.

Holly had been correct in assuming that Becca would want to include the cat in the ceremony. Evan had tried to persuade the little girl that the cat would be a nuisance, but Becca had been insistent. Holly had purchased the basket for her to use, and Evan had finally given up in the face of their combined efforts.

Holly loved Becca as if the little girl was her own child, and she couldn't wait until Gott saw fit to bless her and Evan with children of their own. She was happier than she could ever remembers, and looked forward to the next few weeks where they would be traveling to stay with each of her relatives and his.

"Mrs. Miller, what are you smiling about?" Evan whispered by her ear as she bid another group of guests farewell.

"Is there a reason I shouldn't be smiling?" she asked in response.

"Not that I can think of. Your aunt and uncle are taking Becca with them for the weekend. She seems to like their kinner well enough, and she even talks to them at time."

Becca still struggled with talking about some things, but each day and month Holly could tell it was getting easier for the little girl.

"That is very nice of them," she said in response to her knowledge of Becca's sleeping arrangements.

"Very. We've spoken with everyone and are more than okay to leave at any time."

Holly nodded and then looked around at the barn full of people who had come out to witness their marriage. "Let's go now then."

Evan nodded and escorted her to the waiting buggy. Holly allowed him to hand her up into the buggy, and as word spread of their departure, everyone came out of the barn to wave them off. Contrasts were her thing, and she was amazed as she looked at the people who'd come out to help them celebrate. She'd come to New Wilmington, an orphan and all alone in the world. She'd gained a new understanding of Gott, a familey, and a husband and dochdern in the last eight months.

As they headed for Evan's farm, she placed a hand upon her stomach and ushered up a silent prayer, Gott, let there be a new addition to our little familye ten months from now. A schweschdern or brudern for Becca to play with, and a new little life to love and teach Your ways to.

She reached for her new husband's hand and sighed in contentment. It had taken her a while to get to this point, but she was finally home and secure. She had just needed to find her roots. Danke, mamm for protecting me and I'm sorry if I hurt you. Gott, forgive me for my selfishness and help me never to forget where I've come from. Amen.

Made in the USA
Middletown, DE
25 October 2017